CHAPTER 1

Gracie extended her hand cautiously. She'd read somewhere that horses preferred being stroked rather than patted, so maybe it might be the thing to bring Bobby round. But the piebald pony pinned his ears back and shook his head crossly, as if swatting away an annoying fly.

Gracie slumped, the disappointment building. She *knew* they hadn't known each other long, but she had so hoped to have made friends by now. But Bobby turned grumpily back towards his hay. Moving swiftly out of the way of his sturdy hindquarters, Gracie knew he was telling her in his own pony language to leave him alone.

"Enjoy your lunch, Bobby," she said, hoping he recognised her kind tone. "See you later for our lesson."

There was nothing else she could do. Gracie had planned to spend some time in the pony's stable, to brush his silky mane which was half black and half white, giving him a striking appearance. He

SUNSHINE STABLES

GRACIE *and the* GRUMPY PONY

OLIVIA TUFFIN

ILLUSTRATED BY
JO GOODBERRY

nosy crow

FOR JACK

First published in the UK in 2021 by Nosy Crow Ltd
The Crow's Nest, 14 Baden Place, Crosby Row
London, SE1 1YW, UK

Nosy Crow and associated logos are trademarks and/or registered
trademarks of Nosy Crow Ltd

978 1 78800 824 2

A CIP catalogue record for this book will be available from the British Library.

Printed and bound in the UK by Clays Ltd, Elcograf S.p.A.

Papers used by Nosy Crow are made from wood grown in
sustainable forests.

1 3 5 7 9 10 8 6 4 2

www.nosycrow.com

was a beautiful pony, a gypsy cob with strong legs and feathery fetlocks and a forelock which almost reached his soft muzzle. Gracie had been looking forward to her week at pony camp for what felt like forever, but it wasn't going as she had imagined. And there was so much at stake...

"Gracie!"

Looking up, Gracie turned in the direction of the friendly call. It was Jess and Willow, two of the other camp members. Jess was paired with a lovely pony called Merlin, and Willow was paired with a pony called Luna, who was super-fast at games. But more importantly to Gracie, Luna was friendly, and Willow could throw her arms around her pony without a second thought.

Gracie waved back and crossed over the yard, twirling and skipping as she did so. Her mum always gently teased her about how she couldn't help but dance everywhere she went. Gracie was amazing at dancing and singing and acting, and had attended Miss Duval's dance school in town for years. But ponies were her biggest love.

Gracie made herself smile at her friends, despite her gloom. She was good at *looking* cheerful and confident, just as she did on stage. Since they'd arrived at camp, everyone had gravitated to her. She was happy-go-lucky, kind and a good listener, and had a ready supply of sweets tucked into her suitcase for sharing. But sometimes Gracie felt lonely.

"You've a big heart, full of love," her mum would tell her. Gracie would smile, take a deep breath and ask, even though she knew the answer, "Please, Mum, can we think about a pet this year?"

And her mum would smile and ruffle Gracie's glossy black curls. "I *will* think about it," she would reply kindly. "Just not quite yet, OK?"

Gracie *longed* for a pet. Something to care for and love and call her own. Her friends thought she was super-confident, and would often tell her how amazed they were that she could get up onstage and sing her solos. But deep down, Gracie wanted to be loved for herself, not for her dancing and singing.

She knew a dog was out of the question – her mum and dad worked long hours in their demanding jobs – but Gracie felt sure she could have a kitten. They had a lovely safe garden, well away from the main roads. Her dad, who was really good at making things, could install a little cat flap. But mostly she longed to curl up on her favourite bean bag in the evenings and chat to the kitten about her day, all her hopes, all her fears. She could just be Gracie, without all the stage-show stuff. But so far, her mum and dad had put her off.

Until now.

"I think you're old enough, Gracie," her mum had said, sitting her down one evening. "And I know how much you'd love your own pet, so your dad and I want to do that for you. But a kitten is a big responsibility. You would have to make sure you know how to look after it, how to make it happy. It's a huge thing. Not something you can just give up on if it gets tough. I want you to prove over the summer how responsible you can be. And," she'd paused with a smile, "I've got the perfect opportunity. Have you heard of Sunshine Stables Pony Camp?"

When her mum surprised her with the news that she had booked her into the popular camp, Gracie had been over the moon. She would have her own pony to look after for a whole week, as if he or she was her very own. Then Lainey, who owned Vale Farm, where the camps were held, could give a good report to her mum and dad. And she'd get a week of pony fun too!

Gracie had been riding on and off for quite a long time. Her years of dancing meant she was balanced and confident in the saddle. She didn't have that much experience caring for ponies but had studied loads in preparation. She had even gone over to one of her school friends' houses to spend an afternoon with her friend's mum, who owned a horse. Like with everything she did in life, Gracie wanted to be the best she could be, and this was her big chance to get the kitten of her dreams!

But things had started to go wrong from the very beginning. Lainey had matched each camp member with a pony, and Gracie had been so excited to get Bobby. He'd already caught her eye in the stable's brochure.

She'd immediately given him a hug when they had been introduced, but Bobby had put his ears back and practically shoved her away.

"Oh, Bobby's not very affectionate, I'm afraid," Zoe, the yard groom, who was responsible for the care of all the ponies, had said with a kind smile. "He's not horrid. He just likes his own space. Like us. We're all different, see?"

"OK," Gracie had said in a small voice. "I do see."

But she hadn't given up. Perhaps when Bobby saw how much she loved him, he'd come round! But now she realised that wasn't happening. It wasn't just him needing his own space. He didn't seem to like her at all!

CHAPTER 2

Sighing, Gracie shook her head, brought back to the present by Willow and Jess's chatter. They were talking about one of the fun activities Lainey had planned: a "Decorate Your Pony" Day! Linking arms, the three girls headed towards the camp barn, where Willow had left to get her gloves.

"I'm not sure where I'll find anything to decorate Luna," Willow said, frowning. "I don't know what to do."

"Hmm," Jess replied. "You could plait some daisies into her mane? That would look really nice."

"Oh!" Willow said, seeming to perk up. "Good idea! What will you do, Gracie?"

And suddenly Gracie had her own idea. She had loads of stuff at home she used for dance and stage performances: cans of spray glitter, and feathers and stars. She could make stencils out of a bit of card and decorate Bobby's shiny black patches with glitter and weave the stars into his long mane. She could even make a crown for Bobby's brow band. This was just her thing!

And maybe it could be the thing that bonded her and Bobby. She tried to squash the voice in her head that said Bobby would hate it. He didn't even seem to enjoy having his mane brushed. Gracie felt sure he was getting worse, and that the problem was her. But she had to try. It would just be a case of getting hold of her bag of stuff.

"Ask Lainey to ring your mum!" Willow said when Gracie explained. "Could she drop it off?"

"Yes," Gracie said. "Absolutely."

Having found her gloves, Willow gestured back out to the yard, and she and Jess smiled at Gracie.

"Coming back out?" Willow said. "We're going to practise plaiting."

Gracie shook her head. For a second she thought about telling her worries to her friends but they were clearly preoccupied with their next pony task.

"Maybe later," she said. "I'm just going to sort out my stuff then I'll follow you."

"Cool," said Jess. "See you in a bit."

Once Willow and Jess had headed back out, Gracie sat down on her camp bed. She didn't *actually* have anything to do. She thought she might read *Pony* magazine, remembering an article on trotting poles, which would be useful before their next lesson. But the peace was soon shattered by Sophie, another camp member, flopping down on her bed in a dramatic fashion. Sophie always completed her chores in double-quick time, but Gracie had noticed that she wasn't quite as thorough as the others. Although she knew Sophie adored the pony she had been paired with, a gorgeous Exmoor called Gorse, Gracie felt a wave of jealousy. Sophie could spend hours with her pony if she wanted, but was choosing to be in the camp barn instead.

Sophie looked up, peering at Gracie through her own dark hair.

"What's up?" she asked. Gracie paused. Sophie was known for her wild sense of humour, but she was friendly and seemed as though she was a good listener.

"It's Bobby," Gracie said, looking down at her socks. "Whatever I do, he just seems to hate me."

"I'm sure he doesn't," Sophie replied kindly. "You've only known him a little while! Perhaps you just need more time."

But Gracie shook her head.

"No, I'm sure," she said glumly. "You've all bonded with your ponies – like you and Gorse, you love each other. Everything I've tried with Bobby, like grooming him and spending time with him, doesn't work."

Sophie looked thoughtful.

"You could sing to him? You're great at singing, aren't you?" Sophie tilted her head and Gracie gave a start.

"How do you know?"

"My friend Holly is at your school," Sophie grinned. "She was telling me how amazing you were in the play."

Gracie smiled, a rush of pride making her feel all tingly. After feeling so down, Sophie's compliment really cheered her up. But she would rather be complimented on her pony care!

"Thank you," she said gratefully.

Sophie continued enthusiastically. "Just go into his stable and sing. I *bet* he'd really like it. I read about it in *Pony* magazine. One of the tips for if you are out hacking and get nervous of falling off or something is to sing to your pony. It relaxes you, and it relaxes your pony. So it's probably the same in the stable, isn't it?"

Gracie thought hard. It actually *wasn't* the silliest idea.

"Thanks, Sophie," she said with a smile. "I'll give it a try. But what should I sing?"

"Oh, anything!" Sophie said airily. "I don't think it matters."

Feeling more positive, Gracie grinned at her

friend and stood up, dusting a few hay strands from her camp T-shirt. Heading into the yard, she noticed that most of the ponies bobbed their heads over their stable doors, keen for a treat or a fuss.

There was dear Henry, a kindly dark bay who was ridden by Poppy; little Nutmeg, Amina's pony, a star jumper; and Luna, the super-fast games pony. But not Bobby.

Feeling slightly hesitant, she opened his stable and cleared her throat. Was this a good idea? Sophie had been convinced it would work, so, checking no one was listening, Gracie clicked her tongue, trying to encourage Bobby to look at her.

Then in her clear, sweet voice she began singing the lead solo from her latest school play. But she only managed one line before Bobby spun around, ears flat back and eyes rolling. He snapped at the air above Gracie's arm, and she only just had time to move out of the way.

"I'm sorry, Bobby," she said miserably. "Sorry that annoyed you."

He *clearly* hadn't enjoyed her singing one bit. Gracie quickly let herself out of the stable and Bobby turned back to his hay. If ponies could huff, Gracie thought, Bobby was doing just that! She felt tears spring to her dark eyes and swallowed hard. To make matters worse, Gracie looked over to see the blue estate her mum drove edging into the yard.

Gracie had asked Lainey to ring her. Her mum often worked from home and had been able to come at short notice, but Gracie had hoped her mum would see her smiling and cheerful, and perhaps brushing an equally cheerful Bobby in the sunshine. She had to use her acting skills, and quickly. Wiping her eyes, she tossed her head, drew herself up tall and crossed the yard to meet her mum.

"Gracie!" Her mum got out of the car and enveloped her in a hug. For a split second, in the safety of her mum's arms, Gracie wanted to burst into tears and tell her about how it was all going wrong with Bobby. But then her mum continued, "I've got all your glitters and things," and reached into the car for the bag. "What a lovely idea! Now, I don't know all that much about horses, but it sounds like you've got a real bond with your pony, if he's letting you dress him up."

Gracie bit her lip. "Yes," she said, as brightly as possible.

"How wonderful," her mum said happily. "You know, this camp is a great chance for you to really learn how to take responsibility for an animal!" She gave Gracie another hug, obviously needing to get back to work. "And you're clearly doing a great job. I'm really proud of you, and so is Dad."

Gracie knew she couldn't tell her mum a thing. And she couldn't risk giving Bobby up either. She had to persevere.

At first, as her mum drove out of the yard with a wave, Gracie was too upset to notice the soft tickle on her shins, and the purr which was growing more insistent. Sniffing, she looked down and felt herself smile as she crouched on to the cobbled yard, reaching out her hand to stroke a beautiful cat, glossy black with white paws and huge eyes.

"Hello!" Gracie felt hugely cheered up as the cat weaved around her ankles, tilting her head against Gracie's palm. She was so friendly and so ...

"Fat!" Gracie exclaimed, looking at the cat's tummy. "What have you been eating?"

The cat dipped her head and purred again, as if to say, *Don't worry about my tummy. Carry on making a fuss of me!* Gracie hadn't seen her before and wondered if she belonged to Lainey. She had come to Gracie at just the right time, when she had been at her saddest.

Cross-legged on the warm cobbles, Gracie giggled as the cat rolled luxuriously next to her before batting away a hairband Gracie had found in her pocket. The more attention she paid the cat, the more she seemed to want, but Gracie didn't mind one bit. This was what she had been missing over the past couple of days, she realised sadly. Something that would love her back!

CHAPTER 3

But all too soon, Gracie had to leave to get ready for her lesson.

"Sorry, girl," she said regretfully as she stood up, before reaching down to stroke the glossy cat one last time. "But I'll see you later."

The cat seemed to understand her, and strolled off, before leaping deftly up on to an old stone trough and settling down in a patch of sunlight.

Gracie felt her heart sink as she headed over to fetch Bobby's tack. She had cleaned it really carefully earlier, taking her time to rub the saddle soap into the nut-brown leather, enjoying the shine that was produced by her cloth.

But her thoughts were interrupted as the door opened and a girl with red hair strode in and started looking through all the tack boxes, as if she was searching for something. Gracie wondered if she was a friend of Emily, Lainey's daughter – she looked about the same age. Smiling, Gracie gave a little wave.

"Hello."

"Hey." The girl turned to Gracie and smiled brightly back, but then frowned as she seemed to look closer at the bridle Gracie was holding.

"That's Bobby's bridle," she said.

"Yes," Gracie answered, feeling a little confused by the girl's sudden sharp tone. "I'm riding him at camp."

But before she could say any more, Lainey came in.

"Ah, Gracie, great timing," she said happily. "This is Ellie." She gestured at the red-haired girl. "She has occasional lessons here and now Izzy has gone home to rest I could accommodate another rider. Ellie was on a waiting list so it worked out well."

Izzy was a girl who had started camp at the same time as Gracie and her friends, but had twisted her ankle in a fall.

"Ellie often rides Bobby," Lainey continued as she burrowed around in a box of bits, before pulling out a snaffle. "Aha!" she said triumphantly.

"What do *you* think of Bobby?" Ellie asked Gracie in a tone she couldn't quite work out.

Gracie didn't want to let this other girl know she'd been having a tricky time!

"Oh!" she said breezily, flicking her curls back. "He's great."

Luckily Lainey was distracted, fiddling around fitting the bit on to a bridle. Ellie looked at her and then shrugged.

"That's good," she said, but she sounded disappointed. "So am I definitely riding Merry?" she asked Lainey, who had now joined them.

"Yes, that's right!" Lainey beamed, seemingly oblivious to Ellie's mood. "Always good to mix it up and ride different ponies. But," she turned to Gracie, "as I said, Ellie has ridden Bobby a bit. Perhaps if you need any pointers you could chat to her?"

But Gracie had a funny feeling about Ellie. "Sounds great," she said vaguely. "I'd better go and tack him up."

She could feel Ellie watching her as she gathered up Bobby's kit, and felt her stomach tie itself into knots. It was hard enough getting Bobby onside, and now it seemed as though she had a rival!

"Hello," Gracie said cautiously a few minutes later as she placed the saddle over Bobby's door and let herself in. "Oh," she continued, gently flicking a few shavings off Bobby's shiny coat. "You've had a sleep."

Bobby's mane was so long it was easy to see he'd been lying down. The shavings looked like snowflakes in his black and white locks.

Tying the piebald pony up, Gracie took a brush from his grooming kit and set to work. Was it her imagination, or did he seem just a bit happier this afternoon? His eyes were gentler somehow, and his ears were no longer back. She felt her heart lift. Perhaps her singing *had* worked! Maybe it had been the breakthrough they needed!

"Is everyone happy?"

Lainey was in the middle of the riding arena. She was always dressed smartly – today she wore a white Sunshine Stables polo shirt and navy breeches. As everyone lined up, she gave each pony a pat. There was Sophie, laughing astride the merry Exmoor, Gorse, chatting with Jess on the grey, Merlin. Lainey paused next to Gracie, reaching up to stroke Bobby's forelock. They'd all just enjoyed a great flatwork session and were now moving on to gridwork, a line of low jumps, designed to test accuracy and position.

"Well done, Gracie," Lainey smiled, keeping her voice low. "I know Bobby can be a bit aloof in the stable, but you're riding him really nicely. That canter was lovely."

Gracie smiled back. Bobby *was* lovely to ride.

So smooth and responsive, and comfortable too. Perhaps him being so grumpy was the price she had to pay ... but maybe that was getting better too.

"Thank you," she replied. "I'm really enjoying riding him."

She was thrilled with Lainey's compliment. Things were looking up!

"Woo!" Sophie grinned as she and Gorse trotted back, having just jumped through the grid.

Gorse's ears were pricked as he tossed his mane. "Your turn," she said, her eyes sparkling. "Have fun!"

"OK, Gracie!" Lainey called. "Trot on. Sit up nice and straight, then ask for a canter."

Doing as she was instructed, Gracie nudged Bobby on. It was like riding a rocking horse, she reflected as she nudged her inside heel against Bobby's side. He struck off perfectly into a canter, feathers and mane flying. It felt as though Gracie was flying too as they jumped through the line of coloured poles.

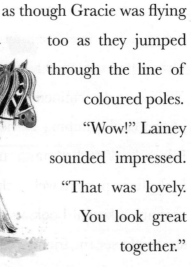

"Wow!" Lainey sounded impressed. "That was lovely. You look great together."

Gracie smiled, feeling much happier. Stealing a glance at Ellie, she noticed the other girl was glaring at her. Gracie shook her head, concentrating on Bobby's black and white mane. If she and Bobby were getting on well now, Ellie would just have to accept that!

Gracie's good mood didn't last. After untacking and brushing Bobby, Gracie untied his lead rope and started to walk him back towards his open stable door. The shavings bed was banked up neatly, and a fresh hay net was waiting for him. Gracie had scrubbed his bucket until it sparkled.

She was determined to look after Bobby as well as she could, hoping Lainey would report good things back to her mum and dad. If she could look after a pony as well as this, she could certainly manage a kitten! Looking around, Gracie hoped she might see the friendly cat from earlier, but she was nowhere to be seen.

"Come on, Bobby." Gracie clicked her tongue. "Look how lovely your stable looks."

But Bobby was backing off, pulling the rope taut. Gracie could see the whites of his eyes, and he looked a bit scary. She gulped.

"What is it, boy?" she tried again, pulling a little harder this time. Bobby followed her for a step before leaping dramatically to the side, wrenching the rope through Gracie's hands. The pain was awful and she instantly regretted taking her gloves off, but her hands had been so hot and sweaty after the lesson. She still had hold of the piebald pony – just – but he was dancing about, throwing his head up.

Gracie tried to ignore her burning hands and gave Bobby's rope one last tug, but he half reared and finally pulled the rope free, careering around the yard, sending the chickens squawking and

Mini, the tame sheep, diving for cover under the mounting block.

"Oh!" Gracie gave a sob. "Help me!"

Amina was the first of her friends to come running, but Ellie was faster, appearing out of nowhere with a feed scoop.

"Bobby!" Ellie called. He was now in the corner of the yard with his head aloft, his nostrils wide and trembling. Ellie pushed her red hair back and approached him, giving the scoop a rattle.

"Now then, Bobby," she said gently. "What's got into you?"

Ellie had no problem getting hold of the rope and, to Gracie's dismay, Bobby followed Ellie meekly as she led him straight back into his stable. Gracie swallowed hard. It had been her – she'd caused him to act that way.

CHAPTER 4

"I've never seen him do that," Ellie said, confirming Gracie's thoughts. "But you know he'll do anything for food," she added, in a tone that implied Gracie hadn't known at all. Zoe, alerted by all the commotion, came over and Ellie bossily explained the situation before Gracie could say a word.

"Silly chap." Taking over from Ellie, Zoe gave Bobby a pat as she slipped his head collar off. "That was very unlike you."

That made Gracie feel worse. She tried to hide her hands as she took the head collar from Zoe, but the groom seemed to notice straight away.

"Oh, Gracie," Zoe said in a kind voice. "I know how much that can hurt. Come on, let's sort you out."

Following Zoe to the kitchen of Lainey's house, Gracie tried not to let the tears that had been threatening fall. Lainey's kitchen was lovely and cool, with beams covered in rosettes. There were photos everywhere of Lainey riding round huge cross-country courses, and of Jack and Emily, her children, on their ponies. A stack of *Horse & Hound* magazines jostled for space on a side table, under which sat Lainey's spaniel, Skate, who thumped her freckled tail. It was pony heaven, and Gracie felt a little better as Zoe got some cream out of a first aid kit and applied it to Gracie's hands.

"Now then," Zoe said gently. "You know what I'm about to say, don't you?"

"Yes," Gracie sniffed. "I should have been wearing gloves."

"Well, yes," Zoe said. "That too. But actually I was going to talk to you about Bobby. He..." She paused as if trying to find the words. "I know he can be grumpy but... Look, what I'm trying to say is that sometimes we can clash with horses. Sort of like with people, you know? You don't always click with everyone you meet. It's nothing to be embarrassed about. We want you to enjoy camp, so if you want me to chat with Lainey..."

Her words hung in the air, but Gracie knew what Zoe meant. Zoe was asking if she wanted to swap ponies. Gracie thought about how wonderful Bobby had been in the lesson, and the little breakthrough she'd had before that, combing the shavings out of his long mane. She felt sure if she swapped ponies it would look as if she'd failed somehow. Then she thought of Ellie's glee. And worst of all, Lainey would have to tell her mum and dad.

"I'm OK with Bobby," she said in a small voice. "I'll try harder."

Zoe patted Gracie's arm.

"OK," she said. "If you're happy."

Gracie stood up ready to follow Zoe out. She gave the kitchen a quick scan as she did so, to see if she could spot anything cat related – a basket or a scratching post – but there was nothing. She hadn't asked Lainey about the friendly cat yet, but she really hoped she would see it later. She needed cheering up more than ever!

Gracie was aware all her camp friends were watching her as she headed out to the yard. She took a deep breath, just like she did just before she went out on stage.

"Always smile," Miss Duval would say. "Then no one knows how nervous you are!"

And Gracie *did* feel nervous at the thought of handling Bobby again. All of her earlier confidence had disappeared, but she didn't want to admit it to her friends.

"How are you?" Jess asked gently, tucking her arm into Gracie's as they made their way over to the barn kitchen for a snack. Grabbing a juice, the girls then sat

down beneath the tree where they had found a horseshoe earlier in the week. They'd excitedly hung

it above their beds, hoping it would bring them luck.

"Oh," Gracie said, trying to sound cheerful. "Good! I'm having the *best* fun."

Jess looked at her.

"Are you?" she said, sounding doubtful. "Even after what Bobby did?"

"He just had a silly moment!" Gracie said, sounding more defensive than she meant to.

She didn't feel like talking. Quickly finishing her juice, Gracie made her way out to the yard, hoping the cat would be waiting for her. But only Mini was there, wiggling her short tail as she hunted for stray pony nuts.

Gracie gave a sigh. It was late afternoon and she had to see to Bobby's stable and top up his hay and water. Taking a deep breath, she made herself unbolt the door and push her wheelbarrow in. She gave Bobby a cautious pat, sweeping a few shavings off his neck. Gracie wondered if he'd had another sleep. He didn't look as grumpy as he had earlier, but even so, Gracie could feel the gap between them widening.

She picked up the fork and started to turn over the shavings, pulling out any droppings she found. Then she frowned and peered a little closer. That was strange, she thought, crouching down to look. There was something in the snow-white shavings in the far corner. A handful of dust and musty-looking hay.

Glancing up, Gracie scanned the stable. The block Bobby lived in was a beautiful building with an old-fashioned hay store in the loft, low beams and the original cobbles on the floor. Lainey had told her that they kept some old bits up in the roof – harnesses and even a side saddle – but hardly anyone went up there because it was a bit of a faff, so they used the modern barn for hay and feed.

Bobby was in the very end stable, and Gracie could just see up into the loft through a small opening next to the external wall. The dusty hay debris seemed to be directly below the opening. Gracie wondered if birds had been making their nests up there.

But now Bobby was starting to flatten his ears again, as if annoyed that Gracie was taking longer than necessary. Hurriedly, Gracie jumped up. If Bobby was cross, she didn't fancy getting stuck in the stable with him!

Jack, Lainey's son, was in the yard as Gracie put away her mucking-out kit. Jack and his sister, Emily, were twins, with sandy hair and a smattering of freckles across their sun-kissed cheeks, but from what Gracie had seen so far, they were total opposites in personality!

Jack was friendly and always willing to help the camp members, filling up water buckets or hay nets, chatting away all the while. But Emily kept to herself and seemed quite snooty.

"Do you want a hand?" Jack grinned as he fell into step with Gracie.

"No, I'm good. Thanks though," Gracie said, grateful for some kind company. But it turned out even Jack knew about her tricky time.

"Bobby's being extra grumpy this week, isn't he?" Jack said cheerfully. "I wonder what's up."

And Gracie felt her heart plummet. Everyone had noticed. Zoe, Ellie and now Jack. There was no way Lainey was going to be able to report anything positive, she thought miserably.

"I – I guess," she stammered. But then she remembered something else. "Um," she said, relieved she could change the subject. "Do you have a cat?"

"No?" Jack replied in a curious tone. "Why?"

"There was one in the yard yesterday," Gracie

explained. "Really friendly."

"Probably a stray," Jack shrugged. "Or our neighbour's."

"She seemed to feel at home," Gracie said, thinking about the way the cat had jumped up on the trough. She hoped the friendly cat had a nice warm bed somewhere. But Jack had moved on. He was full of ideas for the end-of-camp gymkhana, and Gracie couldn't ask any more. She'd just have to hope the cat came back!

CHAPTER 5

Everyone woke up giggling and bouncing around the next morning. It was "Decorate Your Pony Day". But Gracie wanted to pull her sleeping bag back over her head. Her glitters and chalk pens and stars were all in the bag next to her bed, but she had no idea what the morning was going to bring.

"Come on!" Amina called to the girls as they ran out into the yard ready to muck out.

But as soon as Gracie opened the door to Bobby's stable, she could tell the piebald pony was in an exceptionally grumpy mood – his ears were flat back. Gracie didn't even dare pat him, just hurriedly got on with the mucking out. She had no idea *how* she was going to dress him up!

A bit later, at breakfast, Jess sat down next to Gracie with a plate of scrambled eggs and started to dig in, before turning to her friend. Gracie was pushing her toast around her plate.

"Gracie?" Jess said quietly. "Are you OK?"

Almost instinctively, Gracie gave a big smile.

"Of course!" she said in the most cheerful voice she could manage. "Why wouldn't I be?"

Jess bit her lip.

"My stable is near yours," she said. "You seemed really nervous with Bobby. Like you were trying to get the mucking out done as fast as possible."

Gracie's face fell.

"I ... I just try and give him a bit of peace and quiet in the morning," she said, hoping she sounded convincing. "He likes to eat his breakfast alone!" Well, that was the truth, she thought.

"You know," Jess said thoughtfully. "Lainey has other ponies. There's Zebedee, the Welsh Section C – she'd suit you. And Biscuit, that gorgeous skewbald. And you've met Ellie, haven't you? She could ride Bobby a bit. You could ask Lainey ... if you want," she added, all in a rush. "It's just a thought."

But Gracie remembered her mum's words, how you couldn't just give up when things got tough with a pet. If she gave up with Bobby now, her dream would be shattered.

And anyway, there was still something she loved about Bobby. The way his eyes had been gentle after his afternoon nap, how he'd felt when she'd jumped him. She couldn't give up!

"I know," she said firmly. "But I'm OK. I'll stick with Bobby."

Jess raised her eyebrows. "OK," she said

doubtfully, but Gracie shut down any further conversation by jumping to her feet to take her plate over to the sink. She was dreading today, but she didn't want to swap ponies, and she *certainly* didn't want to swap ponies with Ellie!

But Bobby was in the same mood when she returned to his stable. Gingerly fastening his head collar, Gracie led him out into the sunshine and tied him up. Picking up a body brush, she set to work grooming his gleaming white and black patches.

He was remarkably clean, she mused. Not one shaving stuck in his long mane. He had the tiniest amount of hay in his forelock, but that was it.

"Have you not had a lie-down?" Gracie asked him as she brushed. "I thought your stable looked lovely last night."

Perhaps even her mucking out wasn't up to

his standard, she thought sadly. Then, taking a deep breath, she opened her bag and pulled out a glitter spray, carefully pressing her finger down on the trigger.

Hiss!

Bobby shot her a look of horror and leapt sideways. The glitter completely missed his mane.

Every time Gracie tried, he darted out of the way, managing to avoid the glitter despite being tied up. Gracie put the spray back in her bag. It wasn't working. She'd checked with Lainey that it was OK to use and Lainey had given her a cheerful smile.

"Of course!" she'd said. "I use fly spray. He's fine with anything like that."

Except, Gracie thought miserably, when *she* was doing it. Bobby clearly hated her!

Rummaging through her bag, Gracie pulled out some stars instead. She'd planned to plait Bobby's mane and clip the stars in. Bobby glared at her as she started to brush and divide his hair but, gritting her teeth, Gracie carried on.

All around her, the air was full of the laughter of the other girls, and their ponies were looking amazing. Willow's Luna was covered in beautiful flowers, and Poppy had managed to make an amazing rug for Henry, which made him look like a medieval knight's horse. Henry looked so proud and handsome.

To Gracie's dismay, her stars weren't staying in place. Bobby wasn't spooking away as he had done with the spray, but every time she managed to clip one into his plaits, he would shake his head furiously. Gracie was hot and flustered by now. Stepping back, she looked sadly at her handiwork. All she'd achieved was a blob of glitter on Bobby's shoulder and a couple of haphazard stars hanging off the messy plaits.

Panicking, she grabbed the glittery crown she'd made and attempted to fasten it to Bobby's brow band. But, try as she might, she couldn't do it. Gracie flung her hands in the air. It was no good!

"Can I help?"

A familiar, unwelcome voice. Ellie came round the corner, dusting her hands on her jodhpurs.

"I'm all done," she said. "And I noticed you struggling."

She actually sounded quite friendly. Before Gracie could stop her, Ellie had taken the crown and started fiddling around with Bobby's bridle, smoothing his forelock and fastening the crown's straps, before she narrowed her eyes and stood back.

"There," Ellie said in a satisfied voice. "That should do." She looked sideways at Gracie. "Do you want to check?"

But Gracie didn't. If she started to play around with the crown, she was certain Bobby would get really grumpy and she didn't want to show herself up in front of Ellie.

"I'm sure it's fine," she said hurriedly. "Thanks," she added. Perhaps Ellie wasn't so bad after all.

There was no time to do anything else because Lainey was now calling them into the arena. Jess raised her eyebrows at Gracie as she mounted Merlin, who had been transformed into a unicorn, but to Gracie's relief she didn't say anything. Nudging Bobby on, Gracie walked into the arena behind everyone else, wanting to get the morning over and done with.

CHAPTER 6

"Wow!" Lainey clapped the camp members as they lined up. As well as Henry the Knight's Horse, and Merlin the Unicorn, and flowery Luna, Amina had transformed little Nutmeg into a bee, and Sophie had turned her Exmoor pony, Gorse, into a punk rocker, having coaxed his bushy mane upwards with a can of hairspray. Ellie joined the group with Merry, who sported bright ribbons plaited into her mane and tail.

"You all look wonderful!" Lainey said happily, as she patted each pony. But when Lainey reached Bobby, her smile faded a little.

"You look very ... nice, Bobby," Lainey said. Then she looked kindly at Gracie, who sat miserably in her saddle. "All OK?" Lainey continued in a low voice so only Gracie could hear. "I know you were so excited about dressing Bobby up. What happened?"

Gracie tried to talk, but her throat felt thick and lumpy. To her awful embarrassment, she felt a tear splash down on to her saddle.

"He hates me," she whispered. "Whatever I do, he just hates me."

"Oh, Gracie." Lainey patted her knee. "I'm sure he doesn't. I think you two just haven't clicked. Here, have a little ride round, then we'll chat."

Gracie slumped in the saddle. She'd totally failed, and it was the worst feeling in the world. Worse than the time she'd forgotten her lines in the amateur dramatic society's Christmas performance, or when she'd had a sore throat the day before an audition for a part in a London musical. She had wanted to prove to her parents how responsible she was. And now she'd never get her own kitten.

But her morning was about to get far worse. As she nudged Bobby forward, he shook his head, as if trying to dislodge the crown. But Gracie carried on. It should stay put – she'd made it so it clipped round the top of the bridle, and she'd seen Ellie fasten it.

Hadn't she?

"That's nice, Gracie," Lainey called in an encouraging voice. "Ask for a canter in the corner."

Gracie squeezed her heels against the glossy black of Bobby's flanks, feeling the powerful leap forward and the rocking-horse strides. Suddenly she was aware of the crown slipping down over Bobby's long forelock.

Stopping dead, Bobby gave a small half-rear as the crown landed on the sand, before whipping round so quickly Gracie barely had time to grab a handful of mane before she was tumbling through the air, falling to the ground with a thump, right next to the now-crushed crown. Bobby must have stomped on it as he spun around. It was the final humiliation!

"Gracie!" Although Lainey was fast, Sophie was faster, jumping off Gorse and handing her reins to Willow next to her. "Oh, Gracie," Sophie repeated, crouching down as Lainey hurried over. "Are you OK?"

Gracie stretched each limb in turn. Nothing seemed badly hurt – she was just bruised. But her pride had taken the worst knock. Looking over, her heart sank as she saw Ellie now holding both Bobby and Merry. She'd obviously caught the black and white pony after he'd run away, and was now stroking Bobby's nose.

"Yes," she mumbled to Sophie, pulling herself up. "I'm OK." She wasn't, not at all.

"You poor thing!" Lainey said, gently brushing the sand from the back of Gracie's T-shirt. "Come on, take Bobby back to his stable and have a sit-down for a bit. I'll come and see you once I'm done."

Fighting back tears, Gracie nodded. Ellie had walked Bobby over now, and handed over his reins. Gracie noticed she didn't quite meet her eye.

"There you go," she muttered, before turning back to Merry.

Gracie ran her stirrups up so they were tied neatly. She tried not to look at her friends, aware of their sympathetic expressions. Placing the reins over Bobby's head, she started to trudge back to the stables.

"Shall I go with you?" Gracie heard Sophie say in a concerned voice, but she shook her head. She just wanted to be alone.

Back at the yard, Gracie untacked Bobby and led him into his stable, grateful that at least he hadn't tried to run away.

"Oh, Bobby," she said sadly, reaching out to

stroke him. "I'm so sorry we don't get on."

But to her surprise, Bobby turned to her and gave her a gentle nudge, almost as though he was saying sorry back.

Then as she left the stable, Gracie watched as Bobby sank down into his soft bed with a contented sigh. By the time Gracie had put his tack away and tidied up the glitter and stars, Bobby was fast asleep. He looked so peaceful and happy, Gracie thought, wishing things were different. It wasn't just the kitten. She loved him, despite it all.

Then something caught her eye. In the same corner as yesterday was the same debris – thick dust and old hay. Creeping over, Gracie smiled as Bobby opened one eye and then closed it again. Crouching down, she examined the mess.

Frowning, Gracie held her breath, trying to see if she could hear anything, but with most of the ponies out in the arena for the morning's lesson, the air was still and quiet. Gracie looked at the low beams which criss-crossed the stable, beautiful solid bits of wood, and started to wonder. Something was going up into that hole and causing the mess to rain down. She still hadn't seen the cat she'd met the other day. Was the cat up there? She could easily leap from the stable door on to the beams, and then up into the gap.

The stable was so peaceful. Looking at Bobby sleeping, Gracie felt brave enough to move closer and stroke his neck softly. He stirred but didn't move away, instead leaning his neck into her. Gracie let the silken strands of his long mane run through her fingers, enjoying their shared moment. It hadn't been his fault she'd fallen, it would have been scary to have something tumble over his head, but Gracie knew it didn't look good. Had she now blown it completely?

CHAPTER 7

As Gracie waited for the others to finish their lesson, she started to feel a little better. After those lovely few minutes with Bobby in his stable, she was determined, despite the fall, to keep trying. She just had to convince Lainey.

But Lainey had other ideas.

"I'm going to swap you to Zebedee," Lainey said, having called Gracie over for a quiet word. "She's a lovely mare who's great at camp."

Gracie felt her tummy flip, imagining the conversation Lainey would have with her mum. *"Just to let you know, we had to swap Gracie's pony..."*

She could hear Lainey's voice clearly in her mind, and see her mum's thoughtful expression. *"She just couldn't get on with Bobby, I'm afraid."*

"Can't I try with Bobby just one more time?" she stammered, and Lainey smiled.

"No," she said in a kind but firm tone. "This is for the best."

Gracie turned to her friends once Lainey had gone to check over the ponies.

"You'll back me up, won't you?" she pleaded. "I can try again."

But the girls shuffled a bit, looking at each other, looking at the ground, anywhere but at Gracie.

"I think Lainey's right," Jess said after an awkward pause. "Ellie said she's never seen Bobby spook like that. I know the crown falling freaked him out, but he's normally really brave. And before that, all the trouble with dressing him up, and when he wouldn't go back in his stable, and how grumpy he's been. Maybe he just doesn't ... like you." She reddened, as if realising how harsh her words sounded. "But it's not your fault," she added hurriedly. "Not all horses and people get on."

Her words echoed what Zoe had said in Lainey's kitchen. Gracie felt a bubble of disappointment and humiliation rise up in her, coming out as anger. They were supposed to be her friends!

"Whatever," she snapped, turning on her heel and walking away from the girls, wiping away hot, angry tears. Not looking where she was going, she ran head first into Zoe.

"Gracie," Zoe said cheerfully. "I know Lainey's had a word with you. I need to pick up Zebedee's saddle from the menders. Are you OK to hang around here for a bit while I go and get it?"

Gracie nodded. What choice did she have?

"Yes," she sniffed. "That's fine." It wasn't at all,

but she didn't say that.

Zoe nodded, reaching into her pocket for her car keys.

"You're a star," she said. "And, Gracie, this is for the best. Now you can enjoy the rest of camp."

Gracie nodded again, not trusting herself to speak. When Zoe had driven out of the yard, she slumped down on to a pile of rugs in the tack room. She didn't want to go back and hang out with the rest of the gang, not after she'd just stormed away. Plus, they were about to ride again, and she really couldn't bear to see Ellie's smug smile. Instead she reached for a copy of *Pony* magazine, hoping to lose herself in the cheery photo-stories and pony-care tips.

It didn't help. The story was about a girl befriending a difficult pony and winning all the prizes at the show. It didn't happen like that in real life, Gracie thought sadly, putting the magazine down.

She wasn't sure how much time it hadn't appeared back, and the ne still going on in the arena. But suddenly Gr was aware something was happening in the yard. There was some neighing and scrabbling around.

Feeling worried, she headed outside, trying to work out where the noise was coming from. Most ponies were in the lesson or out in the paddock. There was only Bertie, Lainey's retired eventer, and Sox, who belonged to Jade, who taught at the stables. But with a sense of panic, Gracie realised they were looking in the same direction – towards Bobby's stable.

Bobby had been fast asleep when she'd left him, Gracie thought. What if he'd tried to get up and got stuck against the wall? Her heart in her mouth, she started to run. Getting stuck against the wall, or "cast", could be really serious!

...ling his stable, his head held

...thinking, Gracie let herself in.

...oy?" she asked shakily.

...hen she came to her senses. Bobby had already proven how much he disliked her, and now she was in the stable with him and he was in panic mode. She could be in danger! But Bobby paused, and nudged Gracie gently with a soft whicker, and then circled again, pausing by the external wall to let out a high-pitched whinny. His eyes were searching her face. He nudged Gracie again, a little harder this time, but not enough to hurt her. Suddenly Gracie got it.

"You're trying to tell me something, aren't you?" she said. "You need me to help you. But with what?"

But then Zoe appeared, her face full of concern. She must have driven back into the yard as Gracie was in the stable.

"Gracie," she said. "You must come out. Something's obviously upset Bobby. It's not safe!"

But Gracie shook her head.

"No, I think he's trying to tell me … oh!"

Bobby reared, tossing his thick black and white mane, his eyes rolling. He gave another shrill whinny and then spun round, heading back to the same wall.

"Gracie, *out*!" Zoe cried.

She opened the door and grabbed Gracie's arm to pull her away, and Gracie had no choice but to follow her.

"What were you thinking?" Zoe cried. "You

could have been seriously injured!"

"I'm sorry," Gracie mumbled. "I didn't think."

Then, out of nowhere, the beautiful black and white cat scampered across the yard.

Zoe frowned.

"There's that cat again!" she said. "I tried to catch her the other day. But she's totally wild."

The cat jumped up on to Bobby's door and, as if by magic, Bobby immediately calmed, snuffling the cat gently as she padded across the ledge. The cat and Bobby sniffed noses, and then Bobby resumed his spinning. Gracie noticed there was something different about the cat. She seemed agitated, stressed even.

"OK," Zoe said firmly. "I'm going to put Bobby into the field. He needs to be out of that stable."

Gracie could only watch helplessly as, with some difficulty, Zoe fastened Bobby's head collar on. He was clearly reluctant to go. As Zoe led him past Gracie, he stared at her, his eyes deep and searching. He was trying to communicate with her, Gracie thought with a jolt, to get her to see what he could. Whatever it was, she knew she had to try.

CHAPTER 8

"Phew!" Zoe said as she returned a few minutes later. "He seems OK, so I imagine something just startled him. He'll settle down now he's out."

Then she looked up as the rest of the camp members clattered happily back into the yard.

"I'd better go and help," Zoe said. "But when I get back, we'll talk about Zebedee, OK?"

But Gracie couldn't keep still. She anxiously twisted a lead rope around in her hands. Something was up – she *knew* it. Then she looked down as something warm brushed against her leg. The cat! Reaching down, Gracie stroked her.

But instead of the relaxed, contented purring of the other day, the cat yowled, a sound Gracie had never heard before.

"What is it, girl?" Gracie said. "What are you and Bobby trying to tell me?"

Jess came past then, her arms full of tack.

"I saw that cat the other day!" she said. "I couldn't get near her. She must like you."

Despite her worries , Gracie felt a rush of pride. Zoe hadn't been able to catch her either. The cat rolled over and up again, as if asking Gracie to follow her.

Jess then peered at the cat, setting down her saddle.

"Gracie," she said urgently. "It looks as though she's had kittens, very recently!"

All Gracie could do was blink.

"How do you know?" she asked.

"Look," Jess said, crouching down. The cat

stayed near to Gracie, but didn't run.

"Her tummy looks soft, like a balloon going down. And she's feeding the kittens too. Look, her teats are all swollen. My cousin's a vet," Jess continued. "I spend my holidays helping her out, so I've seen loads of cats and kittens. But if they're still feeding ... where are they now?"

And straight away, Gracie knew!

"I know exactly where!" she said, jumping up and grabbing Jess's arm. "Come with me!"

Quickly Gracie led Jess into Bobby's stable.

"Aha," Jess nodded, looking up. "I think you could be right. Are you good at climbing?"

Unlike the cat, the girls couldn't leap on to the beam from the stable door, but Jess was able to give Gracie a leg-up so she could scramble on to it. Crouching on the weathered wood, Gracie managed to lift herself up high enough to peer through the gap and into the gloom of the loft.

As she cautiously pushed her hand through, she noticed a small amount of old hay and dust fell back out into Bobby's stable, which would explain the pile of debris she'd found every day.

As her eyes adjusted to the light, she gasped as her gaze fell on the most adorable sight. A tangle of grey and black fluff ... wide, bright eyes staring curiously back at her. Kittens!

"One, two, three!" Gracie called down to Jess. "There are three kittens!"

"Aw," Jess said happily. "But why does the mummy seem so worried?"

As if on cue, the cat jumped up on to the beam and padded along to Gracie. She still seemed agitated. And, just like Bobby, Gracie

knew the cat was asking for help.

"Jess," she said, feeling a knot of worry. "What if there's a fourth?"

Carefully climbing down from the beam, Gracie began sifting through the shavings with her hands. Jess was doing the same. Their first, awful thought was that the kitten had fallen through the hole and was somehow hidden in the bed, but there was no sign of it.

Suddenly Gracie stopped, putting her fingers to her lips.

"Jess," she whispered, her eyes widening. "Did you hear that?"

Her eyes equally wide, Jess nodded. The tiniest sound, the weakest mew, but coming from where? Gracie thought outside. Jess thought behind the feed manager. But they couldn't be sure, and now they couldn't hear it.

Suddenly Gracie knew exactly what she had to do.

"We can't waste time!" she said urgently. "Jess, can you distract Zoe? I need Bobby, and she mustn't see me."

Jess didn't even stop to question why. Nodding, she headed back out into the yard. Holding her breath, Gracie heard Jess call Zoe over.

"Zoe?"

Jess was a brilliant actress, Gracie thought admiringly.

"I just wondered if you could explain to me again about the feeds you were talking about this morning," Jess said. "It was all really interesting and I wanted to know more!"

"Of course," Gracie heard Zoe say enthusiastically. "Come over to the feed room. I've got a brilliant book you can look at..."

And Gracie gave a sigh of relief as Zoe and Jess headed off, Zoe chatting away about sugar beet and competition mixes. Jess glanced over her shoulder. "Go!" she mouthed.

Quickly, Gracie grabbed Bobby's head collar. An awful thought struck her. What if she couldn't catch Bobby? What if Zoe had been right and he *had* been startled? But suddenly Gracie was aware she wasn't alone. She had a little shadow running beside her as she hurried to the field. The cat!

Bobby was by the gate, as if he knew Gracie and the cat were coming. Her heart pounding, Gracie managed to fasten the head collar over his nose and open the gate.

"Uh, Gracie?"

Gracie spun around. Ellie was standing there, red hair pulled back, hand on her hip. She had her other hand on the gate.

"What are you doing?" Ellie said accusingly. "You've swapped ponies, remember? You're *not* riding Bobby any more."

Gracie stood her ground.

"He's trying to tell me something," she said. "Please let me through – it's really urgent."

"Oh, give it up, Gracie!" Ellie said with a horrid laugh, pushing the gate forward to close it. "Why would he tell *you* anything? You can't even get him into his stable!"

"That's because there is something about his stable he's worried about!" Gracie shoved the gate back, unbalancing Ellie, who swayed a bit. "Get out of my way, *please*!"

Seeing a gap big enough, Bobby burst through the gate, dragging Gracie with him. Ellie leapt forward to try and block him, but she wasn't fast enough. For a split second Gracie almost lost her grasp on the rope.

"Sorry, sorry!" Gracie called back, hoping the gate or Bobby hadn't knocked Ellie, but she had been right in the way!

"I'm telling Lainey!" Ellie yelled furiously, but there was nothing Gracie could do about that now. Running beside Bobby as he powered back to the yard, she just had to hope she was doing the right thing.

Bobby came to a plunging halt outside his stable, where the cat, who had run ahead, was waiting. He tossed his head, his mane flying, before spinning round, never leaving the spot by the wall. Only this time he was on the other side of it. Gracie shook her head. That couldn't be where the kitten was, could it? The wall?

"OK, boy," she said. "Let me get Lainey."

Zoe was still chatting to Jess. Gracie tied Bobby up outside his stable and ran over to Lainey's house, banging hard on the door. Jack opened it.

"Gracie?" he said in surprise. "What's up?"

"I don't have time to explain," Gracie said breathlessly, as Lainey appeared behind Jack. "I think there's a kitten stuck in Bobby's stable. In the *wall*!"

CHAPTER 9

Running, Jack and Lainey followed Gracie back to the yard. Even Emily, alerted by Gracie's frantic banging, trailed after them.

"Here," Gracie said. "There's the cat. She's got three kittens up in the loft, but I think a fourth kitten's in there!"

"*In* the wall?" Lainey said, sounding perplexed. "But that's impossible."

Jack, who had been listening intently, suddenly darted off into the tack room, reappearing a few seconds later with a stepladder. "It's totally possible, Mum," he said, looking unusually serious. "Come inside."

Jack set the ladder against the wall and climbed up on to one of the beams, reaching up into the roof space, just like Gracie had. Then he reached over and gestured at the top of the wall.

"Down there. It's hollow, only slightly. Like a double wall. Me and Josh Harper used to dare each other to climb up these beams and drop stuff down the gap." He climbed down, looking a little embarrassed. "We were, like, eight and it seemed funny at the time."

Lainey's mouth curled into the faintest smile at Jack's admission.

"So there's a gap in the wall," she said slowly, "and, Gracie – you think a kitten's stuck there?"

Gracie nodded.

"I think Bobby has been trying to tell me," she explained. "The cat has kittens up in the roof and he's known about them all this time."

Lainey bit her lip.

"But if the kitten's *in* the wall," she sounded worried, "how do we get it out?"

By now, Zoe had joined them, along with Jess and the other girls. Ellie was in hot pursuit, still looking furious. As she reached them, she opened her mouth to say something, then shut it, as if sensing the seriousness of what was going on. Quickly, Lainey explained the situation to Zoe, who was now looking really worried.

"We need to call the fire service!" she said urgently. "The kitten could die if we don't get it out!"

After that, things moved quickly. Lainey made the call and then all they could do was wait. Gracie had untied Bobby, and she held him as he pawed the ground, uttering little whickers as if letting the kitten know help was on its way. Occasionally he would press his head against

Gracie's as if asking for reassurance that she was helping him.

"I am," she would whisper to him. "I believe you."

It wasn't long before a fire engine pulled into the yard.

"I'm so sorry," Lainey said, rushing forward. "I know you must have fires to put out. But we think a kitten's trapped in the stable wall. It's in real danger!"

"Don't worry," a man said as he jumped out of the cab, followed by a woman and two more men. "We get called out to quite a few animal rescues, and we have special training for this kind of thing. We'll get your kitten out!"

Gracie could hardly watch as the firefighters set up their equipment and started to carefully cut into the wall, removing each brick one by one.

What if she'd made a mistake? What if there wasn't a fourth kitten and everyone was furious with her? Or what if there *was* a fourth kitten, and they were too late?

She was still holding Bobby, who was standing as still as a statue, his ears pricked. To everyone's amazement, the cat was now perched on his broad back, watching intently with her large eyes.

The firefighter who'd spoken to Lainey on arrival pulled out a plastic toy from the gap he'd made in the wall. He handed it to her with a puzzled expression.

"My Action Man!" Jack yelped. "Josh swore he hadn't dropped that down. See, Mum, I told you!"

Lainey nodded, looking more concerned as time went on and the firefighters removed more bricks.

"But where's the kitten?" she whispered.

Suddenly the firefighter paused, gesturing to his colleagues to stop. Everyone leaned forward to watch as, reaching into the wall, he gently pulled out a tiny bundle of fluff. It was far too still. The woman firefighter put down her tools and reached out for the kitten. Gracie felt her heart stop as the woman looked down with an anxious expression. Had they been too late? Had the kitten died?

But leaping down off Bobby's back, the mother cat ran over, mewing loudly. The firefighter lowered her arms, bending down so she could get as close to the cat as possible. Suddenly the little ball of fluff in the woman's hands lifted its head and meowed back, the tiniest sound. Gracie felt her heart soar. They'd done it! *Bobby* had done it! He'd rescued the kitten.

"I think this little one's just about OK," the firefighter smiled. "But I'd get it to a vet as soon as possible."

"Of course." Lainey gently examined the tiny creature. "We can't thank you enough!"

Then she looked at Gracie.

"Gracie," she said with a smile. "Do you want to come with me? I can't think of anyone better."

"There you go, little ones," Lainey said a bit later. She smiled at Gracie, who was stroking the purring cat. The cat was lying contentedly under Lainey's kitchen table in a plush new basket that Lainey and Gracie had bought at the pet shop on the way back from the vet. The four kittens were fast asleep, safe and warm, their tummies full of milk.

The vet had given the escapee kitten a clean bill of health and declared her incredibly lucky. She'd also checked over the other three kittens and their mother.

"We'll leave them to sleep now," Lainey said.

"But will you help me, while you're at camp? The mum seems really relaxed when you're around."

"Yes, please!" Gracie said. "I'd love to."

But there was one special pony she needed to thank first. A real hero!

"Bobby!"

To Gracie's delight, Bobby stuck his head over the door and gave her a soft whicker. His long forelock was full of snow-white shavings.

"You needed a sleep after all that excitement!" Gracie smiled, and then, in a flash, she *understood*. Everything made sense! Bobby had been much nicer after his sleep that one afternoon when she'd thought her singing had done the trick. And yet there had been no shavings on him most mornings, and he'd been really grumpy, refusing to go back into his stable.

"Of course!" she said out loud. "You haven't

been able to sleep properly, have you?" The piebald pony nudged her gently, as if agreeing with her.

"While we were all tucked up in bed, I bet the kittens were making loads of noise!" Gracie continued. "You poor thing!"

It seemed so obvious now. Bobby had been trying to tell her all along!

"How's the star pony doing?"

Lainey was back out in the yard now, and crossed over to see Bobby.

"He's great," Gracie smiled, and she knew there was something she needed to ask.

"Uh," she stammered. "I was just wondering, I mean, I understand if not, but I hoped." It all came out in a rush. "But I would love to stick with Bobby. I know it's been hard, but now I'm pretty sure I know the reason for his grumpiness – he couldn't get enough sleep..." Her voice trailed off.

But Lainey smiled.

"Gracie," she said slowly. "You're totally right! I bet those kittens were extra noisy at night. No wonder he didn't want to go back into his stable! And you were really brave. You knew Bobby was trying to tell you something and you listened to him, even after he'd given you a fright. You acted really responsibly. So, yes," she grinned. "He's yours for camp."

CHAPTER 10

Gracie couldn't stop smiling long after Lainey had left. She no longer had to find other things to do – she could just hang out with Bobby. Lost in thought, Gracie ran her hand over his thick mane. They had loads of lost time to make up!

Suddenly she gave a start as she heard soft footsteps outside. Looking up, Gracie saw the familiar red hair and tensed, wondering what Ellie was going to say. The last time they'd spoken to each other had been outside the gate, when Gracie had pushed past her.

But to her surprise, Ellie shuffled her feet,

reaching up to pat Bobby herself.

"I just want to say sorry," she said, clearing her throat. "You were right. You knew Bobby was trying to tell you something."

"It's fine." Gracie gave her a smile. She realised it must have been really hard for Ellie to come and apologise. "And anyway," she continued, "we hadn't exactly looked like a great partnership up until then, so I can see why you said what you did."

But Ellie's cheeks were now scarlet.

"That's partly my fault," she mumbled. "I didn't attach the crown properly." She hung her head. "I didn't realise he'd spook like that. I'm really sorry. I just . . ." She raised her eyes and looked at Gracie. "I just wanted to ride him again."

Gracie thought about that horrible moment and bit her lip. Yes, it had been awful of Ellie, but she realised how much Ellie must love the piebald pony, just as she did. She decided not to be mad. Ellie clearly felt really terrible about the whole thing.

"It's OK," Gracie said, and it was. But she wondered how Ellie might feel about not getting Bobby back after all. To her relief, Ellie answered her unspoken question

"I do love Bobby," she said. "But actually I've really been enjoying getting to know Merry. She's a cool pony. I can always ride Bobby another time."

Gracie smiled, and the two girls exchanged a hug.

"Friends?" Gracie said, and Ellie grinned.

"Definitely," she said.

"Let's enjoy the rest of camp. And you'll be great with Bobby. You actually really suit him."

"Yeah, you do," said a voice behind Ellie, and Sophie peeped round, followed by Jess, Poppy, Amina and Willow.

"We just wanted to say how brave you were," Jess said.

"And we're all so pleased you're going to carry on riding Bobby!" Amina added with a smile.

"Here's to the best camp ever!" Poppy grinned.

Gracie buried her face in Bobby's neck, a little overcome. Then she turned back to her friends and grinned.

"And here's to Bobby!" she said happily, giving him another hug. She could feel the unspoken bond between them now. Gracie had believed Bobby and seen his true self. And now they were a perfect team!

Gracie's day got better and better. She and Bobby
enjoyed a forest ride, cantering over pine needles
and jumping little logs. Afterwards she gave him
a long groom, combing every tangle out of his
mane and tail. Bobby closed his eyes and rested a
leg, as if enjoying the attention.

Once he was out in the field for his afternoon roll and graze, she headed over to the house, where Lainey was on the phone. Lainey smiled and put her finger to her lips, so Gracie went over to the cat basket, where the kittens were stirring. They were beyond adorable, so fluffy and perfect. She imagined holding her very own kitten. It would be the best day ever!

"That's great," Gracie heard Lainey say. "She'll love it at your farm. Speak soon."

Putting the phone down, Lainey sat next to Gracie. "I've managed to find homes for the kittens, when they're old enough to wean," she said. "I have loads of friends with farms and stables and they're lovely homes. I have so many people interested!"

Gracie was torn. On one hand, she was happy the kittens had found good homes. But if she couldn't have one just yet, then visiting the kittens at Lainey's would have been the next best thing, and now that had been taken away. She felt her heart sink.

"But, Gracie," Lainey continued, "one of the calls I made was to your mum..."

Gracie was jolted out of her thoughts, looking up as Lainey carried on.

"I told her how amazing and responsible you've been – she might have had the tiniest word with me about the deal you'd made when I rang about your kit bag."

Lainey winked at Gracie, who held her breath. *Could it be?*

"She's coming up later..."

Gracie stared at her, a grin spreading slowly across her face.

"She's agreed to get you your own kitten!"

Gracie couldn't speak for a minute as she stared down at the basket of kittens. Her throat felt lumpy and her heart felt as though it might burst.

"I'll let you choose yours first, of course," Lainey said with a smile. "I know it's a big decision."

"Thank you," Gracie whispered.

Brushing off her jeans, Lainey stood up. "I'll also have to ring a rescue centre," she said, "for Mummy Cat. As the vet said, there's no chip or collar, and they weren't able to match her with any of the missing pets in this area, so she's obviously a stray."

Gracie looked up, startled. "Can't you keep her?" she said. The cat seemed really happy in the house and Skate seemed to like her too.

Lainey shook her head. "No," she said, sounding sad. "My husband, Tim ... he's allergic to cats! He's being really good about it while they are here – he's been taking tablets and luckily he's out at work during the day – but we can't keep her or he'll be quite ill. Trouble is, everyone wants a kitten, but not many people will take an older cat."

Gracie looked at the cat, who bent her head against her palm with a little purr, and at the adorable kittens, who were all so soft and fluffy and playful. And she knew exactly which she should choose.

"Oh, Gracie, she's lovely."

Gracie's mum had arrived. Still in her smart work suit, she didn't seem to mind that the kittens were climbing all over her. She giggled as they batted at her buttons.

"Isn't she?" Gracie said. The minute she'd told Lainey what she'd decided, it had felt so right.

The kittens were so gorgeous that she knew Lainey would easily find them good homes. But the cat had found Gracie, and had comforted her when she was at her lowest. Gracie couldn't wait to take her home. There was so much to think about – the wormers and flea treatment, and diet, as well as an operation to ensure she couldn't have any more kittens. Lainey had told her that the rescue centres were overrun with cats and it was the responsible thing to do. The beautiful cat would finally have a proper home, and Gracie would have her friend, someone to talk to once the stage lights had gone out.

"We're so proud of you," her mum continued. "We hoped you'd prove how responsible you were over the summer. But you've done more than that. When you chose the cat, we knew you'd made a really kind and grown-up decision. We'll love having her!"

Gracie smiled as the cat, given a break from her babies, curled up into her lap.

"She'll need a name," Lainey said. "We can start calling her it now, so she's used to it by the time she's ready to go home to you. Like the vet said, the kittens will wean very soon."

And Gracie looked at the cat.

"I'm going to call her Bobby," she said shyly. "Then she'll always remind me of camp, and Bobby."

Lainey smiled. "I think it's *perfect*."

Then as Bobby the cat hopped off Gracie's lap to tend to her hungry kittens, Lainey looked at her watch.

"It'll be time for pony Bobby's tea soon," she said. "Gracie, why don't you take your mum to see him?"

Gracie jumped up, taking her mum's hand.

"Yes, please. Come on, Mum," Gracie laughed

as they headed out of the door and into the early evening sunshine. "Come and meet him. He's truly the kindest, most amazing pony in the whole world."

ARE YOU A PERFECT PONY PRO? TAKE THIS QUIZ TO FIND OUT!

1 WHICH OF THESE PONY COLOURS IS THE ODD ONE OUT?

a) Blue roan

b) Strawberry roan

c) Banana roan

2 WHAT IS A BOUNCE JUMP?

a) A jump with no non-jumping strides in between

b) A jump with bouncy balls as wings

c) An extra-high jump

3 **WHAT SHOULD YOU WEAR WHEN RIDING ON THE ROAD?**

a) A warm coat. It can be chilly out hacking!

b) High-visibility accessories, on both yourself and your pony

c) Matching numnah, ear bonnet and hat silk, in case any of your friends see you

4 **WHAT IS A GRACKLE?**

a) A type of girth

b) A piece of lunging equipment

c) A type of noseband

5   **WHY WOULD YOU CHOOSE SHAVINGS OVER STRAW BEDS FOR SOME PONIES?**

a) Some ponies eat straw beds
b) It looks neater
c) Shavings bales are less prickly to carry

6   **WHAT WOULD A DANDY BRUSH BE USED FOR?**

a) Brushing the pony's face
b) Untangling knots in tails
c) Removing dried mud from legs and body

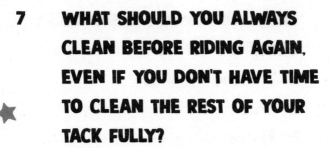

7 **WHAT SHOULD YOU ALWAYS CLEAN BEFORE RIDING AGAIN, EVEN IF YOU DON'T HAVE TIME TO CLEAN THE REST OF YOUR TACK FULLY?**

a) The girth and the bit

b) The stirrups and the seat

c) The stirrup leathers and the pommel

8 **WHAT MUST YOU DO WHEN FEEDING SUGAR BEET?**

a) Feed it only in the mornings

b) Soak it first

c) Add apples to it

9 **WHICH OF THESE BREEDS DON'T GROW "FEATHERS"?**

a) Thoroughbreds
b) Shires
c) Dales

10 **WHEN PERFORMING A DRESSAGE TEST, WHICH LETTER DO YOU ENTER AT?**

a) A
b) W
c) Z

ANSWERS TO THE QUIZ!

Answers: 1c, 2a, 3b, 4c, 5a, 6c, 7a, 8b, 9a, 10a